This book belongs to
....
....

To those little Olympian gods
hiding in our hearts.

The Greek Gods - A Day in Greece © Petita Demas 2018

This is the first edition, published in November 2018
by Petita Demas Ltd
16 Upper Woburn Place, WC1H 0BS, London, UK

Texts by Athina Bali
Illustrations by Chloé Ponthus
Special thanks to Matilda Marcilio

All Rights Reserved.
No part of this publication may be reproduced or transmitted in any form or by any means, electronic or mechanical, including photocopying, recording or any other information storage and retrieval system, without prior permission in writing from the publisher.

Printed in Poland on FSC assured paper.

ISBN: 978-0-9956731-6-8

Petita Demas is a creative studio dedicated to our friends who are small in height but big in our hearts!
Our apps and books are made by parents for parents; we publish the best educational games and books with crystal clear concepts, exceptional aesthetics and strong production values.
Our aim is to strengthen the bonds between parents and children through joyful play and reading.

Find out more and join us on our journey at

petitademas.com

The Greek Gods
A DAY IN GREECE

Texts by Athina Bali

Illustrations by Chloé Ponthus

IN ATHENS. A TRAGIC... COMEDY!

One warm, sunny morning, no surprise there, after all, this is Greece, **Athena** was giving a tour of her city, Athens, to her friends, **Aphrodite**, the Goddess of Beauty, and **Apollo**, the God of Music. They had all visited Athens' monuments before, but this time, as they passed by the Odeon of Herodus Atticus, Apollo had a thought. *"Why don't we put on a play?"*

"Do what?" Exclaimed the Goddess of Wisdom. *"Don't you think we've got enough drama up on Mount Olympus! Surely, Apollo, you don't want more. Right? Aphrodite, help me out here!"* But he did! And so did Aphrodite...

"*Oh come on, Athena,*" said the Goddess of Beauty, who was already on the stage, "*look at this magnificent theatre. Don't you want to hear the echo of applause? Get the flowers and everything?*"
"*Well I'm not as vain as you,*" replied Athena, "*but you do make it sound fun, so why not?*" "*Excellent!*" Said Aphrodite.
"*You'll make a wonderful assistant!*"

"A WHAT?" Athena was outraged! This was her city, the city dedicated to, and named after, her! Plus, this was its most important theatre. So yes, she was going to be the main character! And that was the end of it.

Obviously, Aphrodite was not happy. She was already standing in the middle of the stage, imagining a spotlight on her face, and Hephaestus, her husband, cheering. She claimed that her beauty, and overall presence, would bring viewers from all over Greece. The theatre would be packed every night! But Athena was not having it.

"*Ladies, please...*" Apollo stepped in, "*it breaks my heart to see you arguing, since this play is actually going to have a leading... man! Me.*"
The goddesses looked at each other in distress, but Apollo continued! He started playing his lyre and went on to sing his arguments. *"First of all, la-laaa, this was my ideaaa! Second, I am the artist around hereeee, do you heaaar? I play the lyre and in the viewers' hearts I light a fireeeee!"*

The gods argued and argued, until they heard a loud applause and even louder laughter. *"Who is there? Aeschylus?"* said Athena, *"Is that you? What are you doing here?"*

Aeschylus replied *"What, indeed, is the Father of Tragedy doing here, when this is clearly a comedy? But most importantly what are you three doing fighting over a stage? **Haven't you heard of sharing? Think. What is more important here? For one of you to take all the attention, or to share this experience with your friends? Why not make your friendship even stronger, make memories together?** I think this stage is big enough for all of you to share, don't you?"*

The three gods realised that they were being all silly and selfish. Again! It was not the first time that a mortal, a human, had spoken with more wisdom than the gods. As long as the theatre was standing, it wouldn't be the last!

The End

AESCHYLUS

Who is Aeschylus?

None other than the 'Father of Tragedy', who changed its form once and for all. He added actors, dialogue and emphasised plot. His plays are still appreciated today!

Famous plays:

Seven Against Thebes.
The Persians.
Prometheus Bound.
Oresteia.

IN CRETE. CLEANLINESS IS NEXT TO OLYMPIAN GODLINESS!

What a wonderful day to enjoy the crystal clear waters of Crete! **Artemis**, **Hephaestus** and **Poseidon**, who were spending their summer holidays at the palace of Knossos as **King Minos'** guests, got ready for the beach! Sunscreen? Check. Arrow, tools, trident? Check, check, check!

But, as soon as they arrived, Artemis noticed something strange lying on the beach. She stared at it, alarmed, and raised her bow. It was a slimy, bloated, red and green... creature! Her deer had already started to chew it!

The goddess reached for her arrow and Poseidon held up his trident! The deer looked puzzled. So did the goddess. But Hephaestus, who was used to seeing and making all sorts of objects, took a closer look. *"Well it looks like a giant... slice of watermelon! Except, it's a hundred times bigger! And... inflatable! So probably not dangerous!"*

The other two gods approached cautiously. *"Oh I know"* said Poseidon, *"I've seen mortals on those things, floating all summer long! My poor fish think they're food and get really confused."* *"Well, food or not"* said Artemis, *"once something's damaged, or no longer wanted, it does not belong on the beach anymore. It shouldn't have been left behind to litter the shore."* *"Especially if it's plastic,"* added Hephaestus. Artemis turned to her doe, *"Now my deer, stop eating that! We need to recycle it."*

Without further ado, she picked up the "watermelon" and suggested they cleaned the rest of the beach as well. The gods agreed. Besides, cleanliness is next to godliness!

At that moment, it was time for King Minos to hit the beach and join them! *"What are you all doing?"* asked the king, while still holding his towel and his very own, even bigger, inflatable watermelon! The gods could not believe their eyes. Even the deer could not stop staring! *"I see you're all looking at my watermelon! I had to bring a new one today because the old one deflated and sank somewhere around here yesterday."*

"That was yours?" Shouted Hephaestus! *"You can't just leave things on the beach and expect them to disappear or get picked up by someone else, just because you're the king! Put that down and help us clean. You can start with your old watermelon."*

King Minos apologised immediately and helped his friends finish what they had started.

With the beach all clean and shiny, it was finally time for everybody to have fun! Poseidon had promised to provide perfect waves for everyone to surf and play with, but first, King Minos had to make a promise himself. He swore that he would never leave litter behind again. ***"We must always leave the environment in a better state than it was in when we found it. And we don't need to be gods or kings to achieve that."***

All we have to do is care.

The End

KING MINOS

Who is King Minos?

Son of Zeus, first King of Crete, he managed to take over many of the Aegean islands. He lived in Knossos and it was him that ordered the creation of the famous labyrinth to be built inside the palace.

Mother:

Phoenician Princess Europa.

Wife:

Pasiphae, daughter of Helios.

IN SANTORINI. BON APPÉTIT!

Lunchtime on Mount Olympus meant only one thing...
A traditional Olympian meal, with an extra dash of **Ares** complaining on the side! This time, he was whining at **Hestia**, the Goddess of the Home, who had been left alone on Olympus, with only the God of War, and his famous temper, for company. *"Ambrosia again Hestia? Really? And you are supposed to be the expert on cooking around here!"*

She'd had enough of his rudeness! She would take Ares on a gastronomical trip to Santorini, known for its extraordinary, volcanic scenery, and its unique delicacies.

They hadn't even arrived when **Demeter**, Goddess of the Harvest, on her way back from a walk in the country, heard about the trip. Apparently, news travels faster than even the gods! *"What an opportunity"* she thought, as she was determined to teach the gods the importance of eating vegetables! So she decided to join them and teach Ares some table manners! Or even, come to think of it, some manners in general. Besides, now she could finally take **Euphemus** up on his invitation to have everyone over for dinner, because, *"we should get together around the dinner table more often."*

Euphemus, who was one of Poseidon's sons, and also the Argonaut who created the island of Santorini, was overjoyed to finally have guests and decided to prepare a delicious, Mediterranean meal.

"Mediter-what?" Ares protested! His vulture sighed. The goddesses turned to their host. But nothing could spoil Euphemus's good spirits... Yet! But then Ares started eating... with his hands! He threw down the cutlery, and grabbed at the food greedily. He snatched bits and pieces off everybody's plates, without even asking for permission. He jostled his friends, pushing them with his elbows, and nearly removed them from their seats! He even broke some of Euphemus's finest china! He chewed, and spoke with his mouth wide open, making strange noises, and spraying food over everything! He was not a pretty sight.

Euphemus stopped eating and looked at him, wide-eyed. Demeter didn't have anything left to eat, he'd devoured all of her food as well, and Hestia, who had frankly lost her appetite, decided to put a stop to this behaviour.

"*ARES! **That is not how we enjoy a meal, especially as a guest! You need to think about everyone around you. Where are your manners? Food needs to be appreciated, and so do the people you're enjoying it with. Even your vulture is more civilised than you are. You may be the God of War, but this table is not your enemy.***" When he heard her, he took a minute to think.

He looked at their upset faces, and the chaos on the table, and sighed, ashamed of himself. The God of War took his armour off and apologised. He wiped his face and cleaned up the mess. He promised to replace Euphemus's plates, and before leaving Santorini, he bought himself his very first set of cutlery.

The End

EUPHEMUS

Have you heard of Euphemus?

Son of Poseidon and one of the Argonauts. Once, he threw a lump of dirt into the sea and actually made the island of Santorini! Wow!

Skills:

Thanks to his father he could run over water without getting wet!

IN PELION. DO NOT LIFT A FINGER!

Our beloved royal couple, **Zeus** and **Hera**, took a trip to their second favourite mountain, the beautiful and entirely green Mount Pelion, which they often went to for their summer holiday. They wanted to visit **Chiron**, the most important of the Centaurs, the half-human, half-horse creatures, that lived on the mountain. With them came their cheerful messenger **Hermes**, to keep them updated!

Chiron welcomed them and did everything in his 'horse-power' to make them feel at home, as Greeks do. He gladly gave up his bedroom for Zeus and Hera, and offered Hermes his best guest room. This was actually a stable, what with Chiron being half-horse and everything, according to his guest it was, *"the best stable any god, or mortal, or centaur, could ever hope to sleep in"*.

The gods could not have asked for a more hospitable host! Every night their friend would ask them what they would like for breakfast, lunch, and dinner, and the next day, their delicious meals were ready, even before they asked for them. Wow! Not only that, but a bedtime snack was ready for them at night, and, of course, they were not allowed, under any circumstances, to help around the house! What an insult that would be to their host. They were the guests, after all! They were not to lift a finger.

All they had to do was finish all their food, have another portion if possible, leave room for dessert, smile, and say how much they enjoyed it all. And because they did, it was a piece of cake! Literally! Chiron ran, almost flying, around the house, even faster than Hermes with his winged sandals, as all he wanted was to be a perfect host... even though he sometimes went too far.

"More of that pie Zeus? You only had three pieces! How about some more of that cake Hera? Don't be shy. Here, let me get you a refill. Hermes whatever you do, DO NOT GET UP! What do you need? I know! Another plate of those delicious stuffed tomatoes, right? Anything else I can get for you?"

The gods were having a blast, but it was almost autumn, and they just had to head back to Olympus. They were grateful for everything Chiron had done for them and in order to thank him, they gave him some of their best nectar and ambrosia, and Zeus promised to ensure that the upcoming winter wouldn't be too cold.

Despite all of their parting gifts, they still felt they hadn't done enough. **But for Chiron, it had all been about the pleasure of giving, especially without expecting anything in return. He was just happy to make his friends happy. He was happy to give. He found this to be the greatest and most fulfilling gift. The pure satisfaction of giving with all your heart, no matter how much, or how little, it is that you have to offer.** So, with gratitude and joy in their hearts, the friends parted, but only until next time...

The End

CHIRON

Have you heard of Chiron?

The most outstanding of all the Centaurs! He stood out for his kindness, intelligence, integrity, and healing abilities, this Centaur was respected by both gods and mortals.

Skills:
He played the lyre like Apollo, who raised him as his own son!